TELL ME
A MITZI

by LORE SEGAL

Pictures by HARRIET PINCUS

 SCHOLASTIC BOOK SERVICES
NEW YORK · TORONTO · LONDON · AUCKLAND · SYDNEY · TOKYO

To Beatrice and Jacob / L.S.

To Stevie, with love / H.P.

Text copyright © 1970 by Lore Segal. Pictures copyright © 1970 by Harriet Pincus. This edition is published by Scholastic Book Services, a division of Scholastic Magazines, Inc., by arrangement with Farrar, Straus & Giroux, Inc.

12 11 10 9 8 7 6 5 4 3 2   9   7 8 9/7 0 1 2/8

07

Printed in the U.S.A.

TELL ME A MITZI

CONTENTS

MITZI TAKES A TAXI

"Tell me a story," said Martha.

Once upon a time (*said her mother*) there was a Mitzi. She had a mother and a father and a brother who was a baby. His name was Jacob.

One morning Mitzi woke up. Jacob was in his crib, asleep. Mitzi went and looked in her mother and father's room. They were asleep.

She looked in the living room. There was nobody there. There was nobody in the kitchen.

Mitzi went back into the children's room, shook the crib and said, "Jacob, are you asleep?"

Jacob said, "Dadadadada."

"Good," said Mitzi. "What shall we do?"

"Let's go to Grandma and Grandpa's house," said Jacob.

"Right," said Mitzi. "Let's go."

"First make me my bottle," said Jacob. So Mitzi got Jacob's bottle, carried it into the kitchen and opened the refrigerator and took out a carton of milk and opened it and took the top off Jacob's bottle and poured in the milk and put the top back on and closed the carton and put it back in the refrigerator and closed the door and carried the bottle into the children's room and gave it to Jacob and said, "Let's go."

Jacob said, "Change my diaper." So Mitzi climbed into Jacob's crib and took his pajamas off and took off his rubber pants and took the pins out of his diaper and climbed out of the crib and put the diaper in the diaper pail and took a fresh diaper and climbed into the crib and put the diaper on Jacob and put in the pins and put on a fresh pair of rubber

pants and Jacob said, "Dress me." So Mitzi lifted
Jacob out of the crib and put him on the floor and
she put on his shirt and his overalls and his socks.
She put on his right shoe and his left shoe and his
snowsuit and his mittens and tied his hat under his
chin and said, "*Now* let's go."

Jacob said, "In your pajamas?"

When Mitzi had got on her shirt and her skirt and her socks and her shoes and put herself into her snowsuit and found her mittens and tied her hat under her chin, Jacob said, "Now let's go."

Mitzi put Jacob in his stroller and pushed the stroller out of their front door and along the hall to the elevator.

"Only I can't reach the button," she said.

"Take me out and hold me up," said Jacob. So Mitzi took Jacob out of the stroller and held him way up and Jacob pressed the button. When the elevator came, Mitzi pushed the stroller in, the door closed and the elevator went down to the ground floor and the door opened.

The doorman in the lobby said, "Good morning, Mitzi. Good morning, Jacob."

Jacob said, "Dadadada."

Mitzi said, "We're going to Grandma and Grandpa's house."

The doorman helped Mitzi take the stroller down the steps and Mitzi pushed Jacob to the corner of the street and called, "TAXI!"

A taxi stopped and the driver got out and came around to their side. He lifted Jacob out of the stroller and put him in the back seat and lifted Mitzi in and folded up the stroller and put it in the empty front seat and walked around to his side and got in and said, "Where to?"

"Grandma and Grandpa's house, please," said Mitzi.

"Where do they live?" asked the driver.

"I don't know," said Mitzi.

So the driver got out and came around to the other side and took the stroller from the front seat and unfolded it on the sidewalk and took Jacob out and put him in the stroller and took Mitzi out and put her on the sidewalk and walked around to his side and got in and drove away.

Mitzi pushed Jacob back to the house.

The doorman helped her get the stroller up the
stairs and he pushed the elevator button for them.
They got out on their floor and went in their
front door and into their room. Mitzi took Jacob out
of the stroller and untied his hat and took off his
mittens. She took off his snowsuit and his right shoe
and his left shoe and his socks and his overalls and
his shirt and put on his pajamas and lifted him
into his crib. Then she undressed herself and put her
pajamas on and got back into bed and covered
herself up and then the alarm clock rang in her
mother and father's room.

Mitzi's mother came into the children's room and said, "Good morning, Mitzi," and Mitzi said, "Morning, Mommy," and her mother said, "Good morning, Jacob," and Jacob said, "Dadada."

"Come to Mommy, Jacob," said his mother. "I'll get you a *nice* bottle and change your diaper," and she took him out of the crib and she said, "Mitzi, today can you be a *really big* girl and take off your *own* pajamas *all* by yourself?"

"You do it," said Mitzi. "I'm exhausted."

"Exhausted, are you!" said her mother. "How come you're exhausted so early in the morning?"

"Because I am," said Mitzi. "Mommy! Where do Grandma and Grandpa live?"

"Six West Seventy-seventh Street," said her mother. "Why do you ask?"

"Because," said Mitzi.

MITZI SNEEZES

"Tell me a Mitzi," said Martha.

"Later I will," said her mother. *"Now I've got a headache."*

In a little while Martha asked her mother, "Mommy, now is it later?"

"No," said her mother. *"It's still now."*

In a little while Martha asked her mother if she had a headache.

"No," said her mother, *"Why?"*

"Tell me a Mitzi," said Martha.

Once upon a time (*said her mother*) there was a Mitzi and she had a mother.

One morning Mitzi sneezed and her mother said, "Mitzi! You've got a terrible cold." She took Mitzi's temperature and put her to bed and gave her two baby aspirins and Mitzi said, "Tell me a story."

"Later I will," said her mother. "Now I've got to see what's the matter with Jacob."

Jacob was sitting on the floor, crying, and his mother picked him up and said, "You feel hot, Jacob."

She took his temperature and put him to bed and gave him a baby aspirin. Then she went out into the kitchen and brought Mitzi some orange juice in a glass and a bottle of orange juice for Jacob.

Mitzi said, "Now tell us a story."

Her mother said, "I've got to get you some lunch."

Mitzi's mother went into the kitchen and made a bowl of soup for Mitzi and one for Jacob and when she brought them in, Mitzi said, "While we're having our lunch, tell us a story."

"I will," said her mother. "Only I've got to go and see who's at the door."

Mitzi's mother went to the door and it was Mitzi's father. "I've got a terrible cold," he said.

"I've got a cold, too," said Mitzi's mother.

"I said it first," said Mitzi's father.

"I've got it worst," said Mitzi's mother.

"Where's the thermometer?" asked Mitzi's father. He took his temperature and said, "I'm going to bed. Get me the aspirin, please."

Mitzi's mother got Mitzi's father the aspirin and brought him a glass of orange juice and some for Mitzi and some in a bottle for Jacob. Mitzi's father said he was hungry, so her mother went into the kitchen and made him a bowl of soup and then she gave Mitzi and Jacob some more baby aspirin and Mitzi said, "You said you would tell us a story!"

But Mitzi's mother said, "I'm going to bed."

Jacob and Mitzi and their father sat up in their beds and said, "You can't."

"It's not your turn to be sick," said Mitzi's father.

"Who would take our temperature?" said Mitzi.

"And give us aspirin?" said Jacob.

"And get us orange juice?" said Mitzi's father.

"And make us soup?" said Jacob.

"And tell us stories?" said Mitzi.

"I've got to go and see who's at the door," said her mother.

Mitzi's mother went to open the door and it was
Mitzi's grandma.

She looked at Mitzi's mother and said, "You've got
a terrible cold. Where's the thermometer?" Grandma
took Mitzi's mother's temperature and put her to
bed and gave her some aspirin.

Then Grandma went into the kitchen and
brought everybody some more orange juice. For a
snack she made them cinnamon toast, and noodle
soup for supper, and she took their temperatures and
gave them their aspirins and told them stories and
the next day they were all better.

Only Grandma sneezed. They took her temperature and put her to bed. Mitzi's mother got the aspirin and brought her a bowl of nice hot soup and Mitzi's father made his special cinnamon toast and Jacob took in the orange juice without spilling it and Mitzi told her a story she made up all by herself.

Mitzi's grandma said it was the best cold she ever had.

MITZI AND
THE PRESIDENT

"Play with me," Martha said to her father.

"I'm reading," said her father.

"I'm hungry," said Martha.

Martha's father put down his book, got up and made Martha a piece of bread and butter and sat down and picked up his book.

"And thirsty," said Martha.

Martha's father put down his book, got up and brought Martha a glass of milk and sat down and picked up his book and Martha said:

"Tell me a Mitzi."

Once upon a time (*said her father*) there was a father and he had a little girl called Mitzi and she had a brother called Jacob and they all went for a walk.

Mitzi said, "I'm hungry for some gum," and
Jacob said, "Me too," and their father said, "I don't
have any."

"Well, I want some," said Mitzi.

"Me too," said Jacob, "and I want a parade."

"Well, I don't have one," said his father.

"Look in your pocket," said Mitzi.

Mitzi's father looked in his left jacket pocket and
in his right jacket pocket and in his breast pocket
and in his two trouser pockets and said, "No. Nothing.
Besides, it's almost lunchtime and Jacob always
swallows his. Anyhow, I don't like gum-chewing
children; also the sugar is bad for your teeth and
when that's gone you don't want to chew it any
more. You don't even *like* chewing gum."

"Yes, I do," said Mitzi, "and so does Jacob."

BUY GUM

CHEWING
ON
PREMISES
ALLOWED

29

GONE
TO THE
PARADE

ALL FLAVORS
juicy + non-juicy

NEW
GUM

OLD
GUM
Made
in
1922

BUBBLE
GUM

Beatrice's
Chewing-Gum
Shop

DAIRY PRODUCTS

So their father took them to buy chewing gum but
the chewing-gum shop was closed. It had a notice
up: GONE TO THE PARADE.

"I want a parade," yelled Jacob.

"Me too!" said Mitzi.

"Me too!" said Mitzi's father. There were a lot of
people running and Mitzi's father and Mitzi and

Jacob ran and there was the first motorcyclist going past, and behind him came two more motorcycles, one on the left and one on the right side of the street, and they went past and behind them came two more motorcycles, side by side, and behind them came a great, open black car with one Secret Service man walking on the left and one walking on the right side.

Everyone said, "The President!"

The President was waving to the people on the right and to the people on the left and there were two aides, one sitting beside him and one sitting in back of him, and *they* drove past, and behind them came two motorcycles side by side, and two more motorcycles, one on the right and one on the left side of the street, and then the last motorcyclist all by himself and when he had gone past, Jacob said, "More."

"All gone," said his father. "Lunchtime!"

"MORE!" said Jacob.

"DON'T YELL," said his father. "There *is* no more. It's gone, Jacob!"

"COME BACK," yelled Jacob.

"Okay, Jacob," said his father, "it's time you learned you can *not* always have what you want. Call them back. Go on. Yell!"

"C O M E   B A A A A A A A A A A A C K !" yelled Jacob so loudly that the President turned his head. The President spoke to the aide at his side, who touched the shoulder of the driver in front, who stopped the car. The two Secret Service men stopped. The motorcycles in back stopped. The right Secret Service man ran forward to stop the motorcyclists in front, who hadn't noticed that everybody else had stopped.

The President got out of the car and so did the two aides and they came walking over.

"Did you call me?" asked the President.

"*He* did," said Mitzi. "He's my brother. His name is Jacob."

"Jacob, eh?" said the President. "And what's your name?"

"Mitzi," said Mitzi.

"Mitzi, is it," said the President.

Mitzi said, "And this is my daddy."

"How do you do?" said Mitzi's father.

"Very well, thank you," said the President. "Were you calling me, Jacob?"

"He meant the parade," Mitzi said. "He wants it to come back. He likes parades and things."

"Likes parades, does he," said the President. "Is there any reason," the President asked the two aides, "why we should be going in that direction rather than in this direction?"

"One moment, sir," said one of the aides, and he ran over to talk to the two Secret Service men and he ran back and said, "No reason, sir, why we should be going in either direction."

"Very well, then. I suppose," the President said to Mitzi, "you like chewing gum, do you?"

"Yes, please," said Mitzi, "and so does Jacob."

The President looked in his five pockets. "Do either
of you happen to have any gum on you?" he asked the
two aides. The two aides looked in their ten pockets.
The Secret Service men looked in *their* ten pockets.
The motorcyclists looked in their fifty pockets. All the
people on the sidewalk looked in all of their pockets.

"Fantastic, sir," said one of the aides. "Seventy-five
pockets in the Presidential party alone, and no gum."

"Chewing gum, sir!" somebody yelled. The driver
of the Presidential car had found a piece of gum in
his left trouser pocket, and handed it to the right
Secret Service man, who handed it to one of the
two aides, who handed it to the President, who broke
it in half and gave one piece to Mitzi and the
other piece to Jacob.

"Say thank you, Jacob," Mitzi said.

"Well," said the President, "I won't say goodbye. See you when I drive past again," and he and the two aides walked back to the Presidential car and got in. The first motorcyclist made a U turn, followed by the two motorcycles on either side of the street, followed by the two motorcycles side by side, followed by the Presidential car.

"Goodbye!" called the President and waved as he drove by.

"Goodbye!" cried Mitzi.

"Goodbye," yelled Jacob, and Mitzi and Jacob and their father waved to the President and to the two aides and to the right and the left Secret Service man and to the two motorcycles side by side and to the motorcycle on the right side of the street and to the one on the left and to the last motorcyclist riding by himself and when *he* had passed, Jacob said, "All gone."